DATE DUE			

Dropping In On...
JAPAN

Lewis K. Parker

A Geography Series

ROURKE BOOK COMPANY, INC.
VERO BEACH, FLORIDA 32964

A Blackbirch Graphics book.

Printed in the United States of America.

Library of Congress Cataloging-in-Publication Data

Parker, Lewis K.
    Japan / by Lewis K. Parker.
        p.   cm. — (Dropping in on)
    Includes bibliographical references.
    ISBN 1-55916-003-9
        1. Japan—Description and travel. I. Title.
II. Series.
        DS812.P37   1994
        915.2—dc20   93-47097
                                                CIP
                                                AC

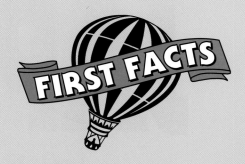

Japan
....

Official Name: Japan

Area: 145,856 square miles

Population: 124,450,000

Capital: Tokyo

Largest City: Tokyo

Highest Elevation: Mt. Fuji
(12,395 feet)

Official Language: Japanese

Major Religions: Buddhism, Shinto, and Christianity

Money: Yen

Form of Government:
Parliamentary democracy

TABLE OF CONTENTS

Our Blue Ball—The Earth

The Earth can be divided into two hemispheres. The word hemisphere means "half a ball"—in this case, the ball is the Earth.

The equator is an imaginary line that runs around the middle of the Earth. It separates the Northern Hemisphere from the Southern Hemisphere. North America—where Canada, the United States, and Mexico are located—is in the Northern Hemisphere.

The Northern Hemisphere

When the North Pole is tilted toward the sun, the sun's most powerful rays strike the northern half of the Earth and less sunshine hits the Southern Hemisphere. That is when people in the Northern Hemisphere enjoy summer. When

the North Pole is tilted away from the sun, and the Southern Hemisphere receives the most sunshine, the seasons reverse. Then winter comes to the Northern Hemisphere. Seasons in the Northern Hemisphere and the Southern Hemisphere are always opposite.

Get Ready for Japan

Hop into your hot-air balloon. Let's take a trip! You are about to drop in on a small country that is slightly smaller than the state of California. Japan is a crowded country. About 125 million people live here.

Japan is made up of 4 large islands—Honshu, Hokkaido, Kyushu, and Shikoku. It also includes more than 3,000 smaller islands, which include Okinawa. Japan has about 200 volcanoes and 60 of them are active. An active volcano is one that still erupts. Earthquakes also occur fairly often in Japan.

STOP 8

La Perouse Strait

RUSSIA

CHINA

Hokkaido

NORTH
KOREA

Sea of Japan

North Pacific
Ocean

STOP 6

Honshu

SOUTH
KOREA

STOP 4

STOP 7

Tokyo

Mt. Fuji •

Kyoto •

Korea Strait

Inland Sea

STOP 5

Shikoku

STOP 3

Kyushu

STOP 2

N

W   E

S

East China Sea

Philippine Sea

STOP 1

Japan

⭐ National Capital

0   miles   200

Okinawa

The island of Okinawa, seen from the air.

Stop 1: Okinawa Island

Our first stop is the island of Okinawa, one of the southernmost parts of Japan. Let's start our visit in Naha, the capital of Okinawa. Naha is like most big cities. It has shopping centers, hotels, and restaurants. If we follow the main avenue, we will come to the sea. Here, beautiful temples overlook the water.

A few miles away is Shuri, a city with a strongly fortified (protected) castle on top of a hill. The gate in front of Shuri Castle is famous. It was built 500 years ago.

In January, the Geisha Horse Festival is held in Okinawa. In this festival, young women wear colorful robes and ride wooden horses in a parade.

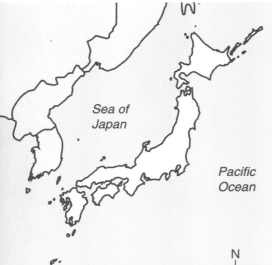

Sea of Japan

Pacific Ocean

N
W—E
S

1 Okinawa

Before we leave Okinawa, you may want to try some of the native food. A typical meal might include *mimiga* (sliced pig ears with vinegar) or *rafutei* (pork with sugar and soy sauce).

 *Next, let's head **northeast** to Kyushu.*

Young Japanese women wear colorful traditional clothing for special occasions.

Stop 2: Kyushu Island

Kyushu is one of the 4 large islands of Japan. The southern end of Kyushu is mostly rolling plains. These plains were formed thousands of years ago from ash and lava. This ash and lava built up from erupting volcanoes. The central part of Kyushu has steep mountains covered with forests. Kyushu looks completely different in the north. There you can see low hills and wide plains.

Naka-dake is the largest active volcano in the world. When the volcano is quiet, you can walk around an edge of its opening, called a crater. If you look down into the crater, you are looking more than 500 feet into the Earth!

There are many rare birds in Kyushu. You can watch black cormorants dive for fish in the rivers. Or you might spot white herons perched quietly beside the many rice fields.

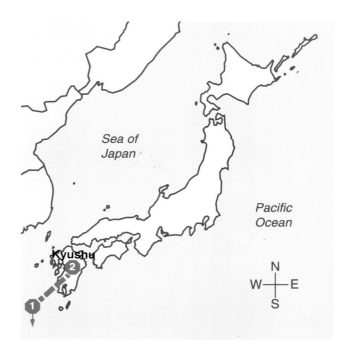

A fisherman weighs a freshly caught tuna in Kagoshima, Kyushu.

Life in a Kyushu Village

Most of Japan's people live in towns and cities. Yet there are many small village communities, called *burakus*, scattered throughout the country.

There are *burakus* on the plains and mountains of Kyushu. Most people who live in these villages on the plains are rice farmers. People who live in mountain *burakus* often raise mushrooms or grow tea.

Villagers eat simple meals. For dinner, they sometimes eat either raw or boiled fish with vegetables. Rice and tea are always served.

*Now, let's travel **east** to Shikoku Island.*

Flowers are sold by sidewalk vendors in Karatsu on Kyushu Island.

Stop 3: Shikoku

The island of Shikoku has a rocky coastline. Fishing villages line the narrow beaches. Here we can watch fishermen pull in fish they catch. On the southern coast, the shore curves inward. Tosa Bay, with its clear blue water, is inside this curve. If we travel north from Tosa Bay, we will see mountains and rice fields. The land then slopes down to the Inland Sea.

The largest city on Shikoku Island is called Matsuyama. It is on the northwest coast. Ferries carry passengers from Matsuyama to other cities along the coastline.

*Now we'll travel **north** to Japan's Inland Sea.*

A fishing village on Shikoku Island looks out onto Tosa Bay.

The sun sets over the Inland Sea of Japan.

Stop 4: Japan's Inland Sea

Japan's Inland Sea is up to 40 miles wide and is 270 miles long. Three of Japan's 4 largest islands border the Inland Sea. Honshu is at its north. Shikoku and Kyushu are to its south and west. The Inland Sea is also dotted with dozens of tiny islands. Very few people live on these islands. When the June rains start, you can barely see the islands through the thick mist.

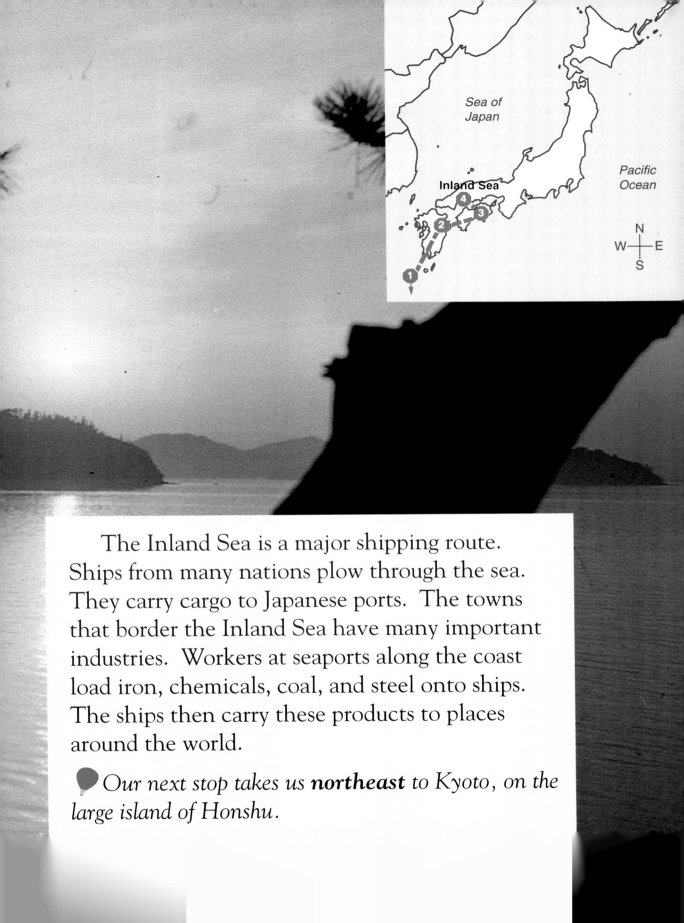

Sea of
Japan

Pacific
Ocean

Inland Sea

The Inland Sea is a major shipping route. Ships from many nations plow through the sea. They carry cargo to Japanese ports. The towns that border the Inland Sea have many important industries. Workers at seaports along the coast load iron, chemicals, coal, and steel onto ships. The ships then carry these products to places around the world.

*Our next stop takes us **northeast** to Kyoto, on the large island of Honshu.*

Stop 5: Kyoto

You will notice that Kyoto is a large city far from the sea. More than 1 million people live in Kyoto. It sits on a plain and is bordered by many green hills.

Kyoto has more than 1,500 temples and shrines. Many stand along the Old Canal. This waterway runs through Kyoto. Cherry trees shade the canal. One of the most famous shrines here is the Silver Pavilion. It is a Zen Buddhist temple. The main courtyard has a beautiful sand garden.

*Now we will travel **east** to Mt. Fuji.*

*The beautiful Kinkakuji Temple
in Kyoto appears to float on the water.*

Sea of
Japan

Kyoto

Pacific
Ocean

N
W   E
S

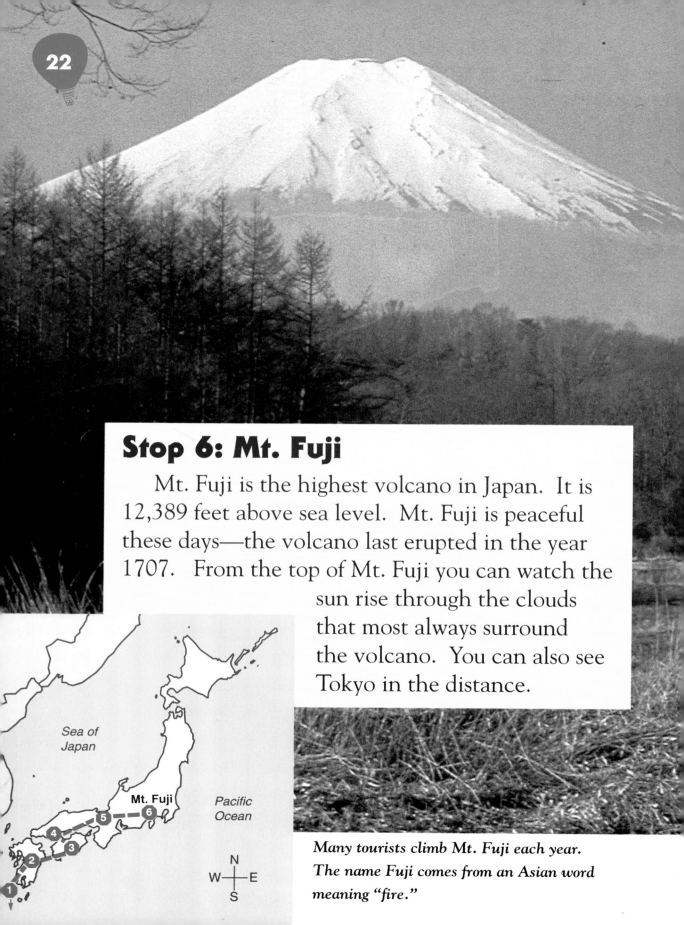

Stop 6: Mt. Fuji

Mt. Fuji is the highest volcano in Japan. It is 12,389 feet above sea level. Mt. Fuji is peaceful these days—the volcano last erupted in the year 1707. From the top of Mt. Fuji you can watch the sun rise through the clouds that most always surround the volcano. You can also see Tokyo in the distance.

Sea of Japan

Mt. Fuji

Pacific Ocean

Many tourists climb Mt. Fuji each year. The name Fuji comes from an Asian word meaning "fire."

Special Foods of Japan

Japan has foods that are not found anywhere else. Fish sold in Japan is fresh, so it's safe to eat raw. *Sashimi* is raw fish. It is sliced so that it looks delicious and is placed

Sushi *is a popular food in Japan.*

neatly on a plate. Another dish is *sushi*. It is rice that has been seasoned with vinegar. Sometimes *sushi* has raw fish in the middle and is wrapped in seaweed. This is called a *nori* roll.

There are dozens of different kinds of noodles made in Japan. One of the most popular is *udon*. These are flat white noodles made of wheat. They are chewy, and you can dip them in soy sauce. You can also add bean curd (*tofu*) to noodles. *Tofu* is formed into a white cake. Sometimes *tofu* cakes are chopped into cubes and added to soup.

From Mt. Fuji we'll move on to Tokyo. For this journey, we will travel **northeast.**

Stop 7: Tokyo

Tokyo, the capital of Japan, is a huge city. Its streets are always crowded. More than 8 million people live and work here. Another 20 million people live in the surrounding areas. Tokyo is really a group of cities and towns. They have

The Tokyo skyline is dotted with modern skyscrapers.

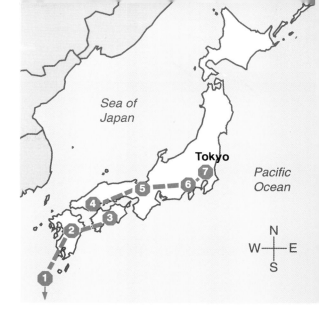

grown close to one another to form one huge urban area.

Much of Tokyo is a modern city with skyscrapers and department stores. Some parts of the city are very old. In these

areas, you will find streets that are lined with wooden houses.

In the middle of Tokyo is the Imperial Palace. This is where the emperor lives. It is surrounded by a large moat and park. The major shopping area is called the Ginza. You can see lots of neon lights here.

Visitors to the Buddha statue decorate the base with flowers.

LET'S TAKE TIME OUT

Growing Up in Japan

Kids in Japan go to school 6 days a week. School usually starts at 7:30 A.M. and usually ends at 4:30 P.M. Students learn to speak Japanese and to write the 4 sets of symbols of their language. They also learn English.

These Japanese children are dressed for the New Year celebration.

Japanese children must take hard tests every year. If a child misses a day of school, his or her mother must sit in the classroom and take notes. After school, many kids go to another school called a *juku*. These extra classes help them do well on their tests.

When people go home, they must take off their shoes before they enter the house. Inside the house, they wear slippers or socks. Most rooms are covered with *tatami*. These are thick mats made of rice straw. Sliding paper screens called *shoji* separate the rooms of the house. At night, thick mattresses called *futons* are placed on the *tatami*.

Now we will travel **north** *to Hokkaido, our last stop.*

Two snow monkeys, called macaques, hug to keep warm in the snow.

Stop 8: Hokkaido

Hokkaido is the northernmost Japanese island. Most of it is covered by forests and mountains.

Hokkaido does not have many big cities. Most people do not like the cold, snowy winters of this region.

Hokkaido has many wilderness areas. The island has national parks with all kinds of wildlife. Sea lions, snow monkeys, foxes, bear, and deer live in Hokkaido's parks.

One of the most beautiful parks is Shiretoko Park on Shiretoko Peninsula. The shore is rocky.

Many tourists come to Hokkaido to see the Ainu. The Ainu are the native people who once lived throughout old Japan. There are probably fewer than 200 Ainu left in Japan, and their way of life is slowly vanishing.

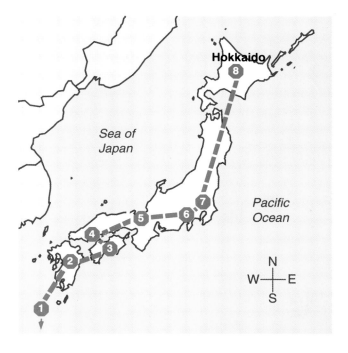

Japan's Many Colorful Festivals

Two young women wear costumes for the Festival of Historic Time.

The Japanese people hold wonderful festivals all year. The New Year in Japan is not just one day—it lasts several days. This is a special time of starting new things. People clean their houses until they shine. Old clothes and other things that are worn out are replaced.

A spring celebration is called *setsuban*. *Setsuban* celebrates the end of winter. On that day, beans are tossed. Japanese people say, "Out with demons, in with good fortune." Each person is supposed to eat one bean for each year of his or her life. This brings good luck.

Children take part in the Flower Festivals of May. Small Buddha statues are covered with beautiful flowers. Children pour tea over the statues. Then they take the statues home as gifts.

Now it's time to set sail for home. When you return, you can think back on the wonderful adventure you had in Japan.

Glossary

Buddha The founder of Buddhism, an Eastern religion.

buraku A small Japanese village community.

cargo Goods carried by a ship, plane, or vehicle.

courtyard An open area surrounded by walls or buildings.

crater An opening at the mouth of a volcano.

island A body of land entirely surrounded by water.

moat A deep hole, usually filled with water, surrounding a structure.

shrine A holy place often set aside for the worship of a sacred being.

temple A building for the worship of a god or gods.

Further Reading

Coates, Bryan E. *Japan*. New York: Franklin Watts, 1991.

Haskins, Jim. *Count Your Way Through Japan*. Minneapolis, MN: Carolrhoda Books, 1987.

Kalman, Bobbie. *Japan: The Land*. New York: Crabtree, 1989.

_____. *Japan: The Culture*. New York: Crabtree, 1989.

Takeshita, Jiro. *Food in Japan*. Vero Beach, FL: Rourke, 1989.

Index

Acknowledgments and Photo Credits
Cover: ©Carl Purcell/Photo Researchers, Inc.; pp. 4, 6: National Aeronautics and Space Administration; pp. 10, 11, 21, 22, 23: ©Japan National Tourist Organization; p. 13: ©Robert A. Isaacs/Photo Researchers, Inc.; p. 15: ©Fenno Jacobs/Photo Researchers, Inc.; p. 17: ©Arthur Tress/Photo Researchers, Inc.; p. 18: ©Lawrence L. Smith/Photo Researchers, Inc.; p. 24: ©Paolo Koch/Photo Researchers, Inc.; p. 26: ©Daniel Nichols/Liaison International; pp. 27, 30: ©Alain Evrard/Photo Researchers, Inc.; p. 28: ©Akira Uchiyama/Photo Researchers, Inc.
Maps by Blackbirch Graphics, Inc.